THE HISTORY OF INCARCERATION

Incarceration Issues:
Punishment, Reform, and Rehabilitation

TITLE LIST

THE HISTORY OF INCARCERATION

by Roger Smith

Mason Crest Publishers
Philadelphia

Mason Crest Publishers Inc.
370 Reed Road
Broomall, Pennsylvania 19008
(866) MCP-BOOK (toll free)

First printing
1 2 3 4 5 6 7 8 9 10

Library of Congress Cataloging-in-Publication Data

Smith, Roger, 1959 Aug. 15–
  The history of incarceration / by Roger Smith.
    p. cm. — (Incarceration issues)
  Includes index.
  ISBN 1-59084-985-X   ISBN 1-59084-984-1 (series)
  ISBN 978-1-59084-985-9   ISBN 978-1-59084-984-2 (series)

  1. Imprisonment—History—Juvenile literature. 2. Punishment—History—Juvenile literature. 3. Prisons—History—Juvenile literature. I. Title. II. Series.
  HV8705.S65 2007
  365'.9—dc22

                        2006002232

Interior design by MK Bassett-Harvey.
Interiors produced by Harding House Publishing Service, Inc.
www.hardinghousepages.com

Cover design by Peter Spires Culotta.

Printed in India by Quadra Press.

Contents

INTRODUCTION

by Larry E. Sullivan, Ph.D.

Prisons will be with us as long as we have social enemies. We will punish them for acts that we consider criminal, and we will confine them in institutions.

Prisons have a long history, one that fits very nicely in the religious context of sin, evil, guilt, and expiation. In fact, the motto of one of the first prison reform organizations was "Sin no more." Placing offenders in prison was, for most of the history of the prison, a ritual for redemption through incarceration; hence the language of punishment takes on a very theological cast. The word "penitentiary" itself comes from the religious concept of penance. When we discuss prisons, we are dealing not only with the law but with very strong emotions and reactions to acts that range from minor or misdemeanor crimes to major felonies like murder and rape.

Prisons also reflect the level of the civilizing process through which a culture travels, and it tells us much about how we treat our fellow human beings. The great nineteenth-century Russian author Fyodor Dostoyevsky, who was a political prisoner, remarked, "The degree of civilization in a society can be measured by observing its prisoners." Similarly, Winston Churchill, the great British prime minister during World War II, said that the "treatment of crime and criminals is one of the most unfailing tests of civilization of any country."

Since the very beginnings of the American Republic, we have attempted to improve and reform the way we imprison criminals. For much of the history of the American prison, we tried to rehabilitate or modify the criminal behavior of offenders through a variety of treatment programs. In the last quarter of the twentieth century, politicians and citizens alike realized that this attempt had failed, and we began passing stricter laws, imprisoning people for longer terms and building more prisons. This movement has taken a great toll on society. Approximately two million people are behind bars today. This movement has led to the

overcrowding of prisons, worse living conditions, fewer educational programs, and severe budgetary problems. There is also a significant social cost, since imprisonment splits families and contributes to a cycle of crime, violence, drug addiction, and poverty.

All these are reasons why this series on incarceration issues is extremely important for understanding the history and culture of the United States. Readers will learn all facets of punishment: its history; the attempts to rehabilitate offenders; the increasing number of women and juveniles in prison; the inequality of sentencing among the races; attempts to find alternatives to incarceration; the high cost, both economically and morally, of imprisonment; and other equally important issues. These books teach us the importance of understanding that the prison system affects more people in the United States than any institution, other than our schools.

CHAPTER 1.

Law & Order bce: Punishment and Incarceration in the Ancient World

The man cowered in the dust, his arms covering his head. He whimpered prayers for protection as the stones cut his flesh and broke his bones, slowly, painfully taking his life. The crowd continued throwing, taunting as they did so: "Traitor! Rebel! This is what you get for plotting against the King!" Naboth could barely speak, but he tried to be heard above the shouts: "I am innocent, it is all a lie!" Nonetheless, the stoning continued until Naboth's corpse lay still on the desert, his blood forming clumps in the sand. The crowd quieted, then left.

Not far away, King Ahab and Queen Jezebel stood inside a tower on the city walls. Their fortress atop the city of Jerusalem afforded a clear view of the stoning. Ahab seemed troubled by the deed. He looked at his wife. "Do you think anyone suspects?"

The queen chuckled softly. "No one suspects. I paid the men well to conspire against Naboth. You can take his field now, just as you wished. As far as the people of Israel are concerned, justice has been served."

The Bible, in 1 Kings 21, records this case of how kings executed and abused the law in the ancient **Near East.** When King Ahab desired the field of his neighbor Naboth, Naboth refused to sell the field, basing his decision on an ancient law that prohibited the permanent sale of ancestral property. Queen Jezebel took matters into her own hands and hired men to accuse Naboth of conspiracy against the king. The punishment for conspiracy was death by stoning. Once Naboth was dead, the king could take what he wanted.

LEGAL PUNISHMENT AND INCARCERATION IN THE ANCIENT WORLD AND TODAY

This biblical account contains several lessons that can be applied to the history of punishment and incarceration.

First, it shows that our modern ideas of legal punishment differ markedly from those of the ancient world. In the United States in the twenty-first century, the government punishes most crimes by incarceration (rather than stoning or some other act of violence). U.S. citizens think, "Break the law, and go to jail." (Most other countries, including Canada, are less likely to sentence offenders to jail or prison, preferring probation, community service, or drug-rehabilitation programs.) In the ancient world, however, long incarcerations seldom took place. There were

Stoning was a common form of punishment in biblical days.

few jails, and ancient rulers designed the few that existed to hold inmates for short lengths of time until they were executed, tortured, or released. Whereas prison sentences are the most common means of punishment in the United States today, death, torture, humiliation, and banishment were the common forms of justice in the ancient world. Some societies (including ancient Israel) had no jails or prisons.

The humiliation of the stocks was common in early America.

The biblical story also shows that the ancient world had codes of law, just as the modern world does. Like today's laws, these codes were complex, and in some cases they contained "mandatory sentences"—laws that required a certain sentence for specific crimes. In the case of Israel versus Naboth, treason against the king required punishment by stoning.

Finally, this case shows that in the ancient world, as in the modern one, justice may go awry. Israel's rulers sentenced Naboth to death, yet he was an innocent victim of a royal conspiracy. Throughout the ages, governments have used incarceration and punishment for a wide variety of purposes. In the ancient world—and in some cases today—political rulers could imprison, torture, or kill their opponents (sometimes simply people they dislike) on a whim. In the twentieth century, the Nazis and Soviet Union incarcerated and killed millions of innocent victims in death camps and the *Gulag*. Even in democracies such as Canada and the United States, courts and judges sometimes err, a fact proven by occasional cases of prisoners (including some on death row) who are later *acquitted* of their crimes.

DATING SYSTEMS & THEIR MEANING

You might be accustomed to seeing dates expressed with the abbreviations BC or AD, as in the year 1000 BC or the year AD 1900. For centuries, this dating system has been the most common in the Western world. However, since BC and AD are based on Christianity (BC stands for Before Christ and AD stands for *anno Domini*, Latin for "in the year of our Lord"), many people now prefer abbreviations that people from all religions can be comfortable using. The abbreviations BCE (meaning Before Common Era) and CE (meaning Common Era) mark time in the same way as BC and AD (for example, 1000 BC is the same year as 1000 BCE, and AD 1900 is the same year as 1900 CE), but BCE and CE do not have the same religious overtones as BC and AD.

ANCIENT ASSYRIA—
THE ROOTS OF LAW

Historians tell us civilization began in the Fertile Crescent (that portion of the world today known as Iraq and Iran). This region gave birth to the Babylonian and Assyrian empires, and these civilizations provide the earliest law codes known in history.

In 1909, French archaeologists digging at the ancient city of Susa unearthed an eight-foot (2.4-meter) piece of polished black rock covered with ancient Babylonian writing. Translators went to work and soon announced the rock was a law code containing 282 different rules and regulations given by the Babylonian king Hammurabi around the year 1700

BCE. Prior to this discovery, many scholars had assumed the Old Testament (the Hebrew Bible) contained the very first laws known to humankind, but Hammurabi's law code proved law originated before the establishment of ancient Israel.

In the past century, archaeologists have found legal texts even more ancient than that of Hammurabi, but Hammurabi's law code is still the earliest example of an important legal principle—that the laws of a nation exist on their own, apart from national leaders. In earlier codes, laws depended on the desires of the king. Whatever an ancient ruler wanted became law; and the king could change such laws any time. Hammurabi's law code, however, outlined national principles of justice, and these laws of Babylon were true whether the king liked them or not. This was a vital development in law and order. Our modern understanding of law assumes the laws of a government are more important than opinions of rulers; even government leaders are subject to the law.

Hammurabi's law code does not mention incarceration, suggesting jails or prisons were nonexistent at the time. However, it does provide a range of legal punishments that applied to various crimes. Death was the punishment for kidnapping, stealing from the king, and a host of other offenses. Lesser crimes, such as theft of a pig, required the thief to make restitution—payment for the stolen property plus additional fines for his crime.

Hammurabi's code provided a variety of different techniques to investigate crimes. When faced with a dispute over property, a judge would question both sides of the argument and choose between them based on their answers. Here, again, the code establishes an important law principle: the right to a "legal trial." This is still followed in most nations today. However, other ancient legal cases were resolved by resorting to other methods. If hearings before a judge did not decide a case, officers threw the accused into a raging river; if he swam to the other side successfully, authorities judged him the winner in the case, and if he drowned, they believed the gods had declared him guilty. Apparently, ancient Babylonians never suspected that in this case, swimming ability rather than divine justice might carry more weight.

An ancient portrayal of King Hammurabi

Ancient Babylon was a sophisticated city, but it lacked the concept of equality for all people.

The Code of Hammurabi is very different from the laws of modern nations in one important aspect. Today, most law codes assume the principle of "equal justice." Ideally, a poor, uneducated person and a wealthy member of the government should be judged and punished in the same way if they commit the same crime. Contrasting with this modern belief, the laws of ancient Babylon gave kings and nobles more power and protection than workers or slaves. Killing a slave was a minor crime, but killing a noble was a terrible one; stealing from a worker was punished only slightly, but stealing from the king resulted in swift death. The ancient Babylonians would have laughed at the idea that "all men are created equal."

ANCIENT ISRAEL— UNIVERSAL LAW

The Bible contains the second-most-ancient set of laws. In some ways, the Hebrew Bible (the Christian Old Testament) is similar to ideas set forth by Hammurabi. For example, both Babylonians and ancient Jews followed the principle "an eye for an eye, a tooth for a tooth" when one person injured another. However, the Hebrew Bible advanced further the notion that law depends on unchanging principles.

The Ten Commandments, which the Bible says God delivered directly to Moses, contain standards that supposedly apply to all humans. The Ten Commandments differ from the laws of Hammurabi in that they claim to be more than just national laws; instead, they state what is right or wrong for all humanity (You shall not kill. You shall not commit adultery. You shall not steal. . . .), without giving specific instructions for convicting and punishing those who break these laws. The Hebrew Bible thus provided another important step in the development of modern law: the belief that some things are always right or always wrong for all people— the concept of "moral absolutes."

At the same time, the Hebrew Bible did contain specific laws and punishments in what scholars refer to as the "Covenant Code." As in Babylonian law, however, the Hebrew Bible says nothing about incarceration for citizens of Israel. Scholars have suggested one reason for this is Israel's early history. The Israelites spent forty years migrating across the desert en route from Egypt to Palestine, where they eventually settled.

A seventeenth-century artist's portrayal of God banishing Cain for his brother's murder.

BIBLICAL ESSENTIAL GOALS OF LAW

The Bible illustrates three goals for punishment or incarceration that still underlie modern concepts of justice. For centuries, various societies have based arguments for differing forms of punishment or incarceration on these principles.

1. *Retribution*: the concept that crime creates an imbalance in the world that must be restored by treating the criminal in the same manner he treated the victim. This is summed up in the famous saying, "an eye for an eye, a tooth for a tooth" (Exodus 21:24).
2. *Deterrence*: the belief that punishing criminals stops potential criminals from committing similar crimes. Old Testament law says that if people witness a public stoning, "all Israel shall hear and fear and never again do any such wickedness as this" (Deuteronomy 13:11).
3. *Rehabilitation*: a concept added by Jesus in the New Testament that sets a goal of changing the offender's character so he will not commit crimes again. In John 8, Jesus argues against the death penalty for a woman caught in adultery, and then he tells her, "Go and sin no more."

During these years, they lived as nomads, setting up tents in different places as they migrated, lacking any permanent cities. In such conditions, jails or prisons were impossible to maintain.

Like the Babylonians, the people of ancient Israel used a variety of legal punishments. Crimes including murder, rape, treason, **blasphemy**, and telling lies in God's name were punished by death. The most common form of **capital punishment** was stoning. The entire tribe sentenced

a criminal, and they all participated in her execution, thus reinforcing the idea that each person had a stake in community justice. Another form of punishment was banishment. According to the book of Genesis, God directly punished the first murderer, Cain, by banishing him rather than taking his life. Crimes against property required compensation—a thief had to return stolen goods and pay the owner something more than what he stole.

ANCIENT EGYPT—THE LAWS OF PHARAOH AND PRISON LABOR

Ancient Egyptians based their lives on the concept of *ma'at*—a word that can be translated as "balance" or "justice." This gave them a strong sense of law and order, yet archaeologists have found no ancient Egyptian law codes. Egyptians regarded their pharaoh as a god reigning on earth, and they believed the life of the nation depended on him. Therefore, the pharaoh was the source of law and order, creating laws and ordering punishments as he saw fit, guided by the principle of ma'at.

Like the Babylonians and Israelites, ancient Egyptians depended on a variety of punishments, rather than incarceration, to support their laws. Lesser crimes demanded public whippings or branding as punishment. These punishments were designed to deter crime not only because of the physical pain involved, but because the stripes or brand marks on a criminal's body were a permanent source of shame in a culture that valued order so highly. Some criminals were punished by mutilation—removing an ear, an eye, or a hand. Egyptian rulers punished more serious crimes by skewering criminals on stakes, burning them alive, or **decapitation**.

Ancient Egyptians did invent an institution important to the history of **penology**: they are the first people known to make an incarceration facility, the "Great Prison" in ancient Thebes (modern day Luxor). The

Ancient Egyptian kings were the first to use forced labor as a punishment.

biblical book of Genesis says the Egyptians imprisoned the Jewish hero Joseph in this facility. The Great Prison at Thebes was a workhouse, where guards forced prisoners to work for the pharaoh during their confinement. Forced labor is another idea that has continued until today. Most inmates in the United States perform some manner of work, often for little more than a dollar an hour, producing goods for corporations that include McDonald's, Microsoft, and Eddie Bauer.

ANCIENT GREECE—TRIAL BY JURY AND DIFFERING LEVELS OF INCARCERATION IN THE FIRST DEMOCRACY

Schoolchildren learn how much our culture owes to the Greeks: democracy, mathematics, geometry, music, sculptures, and so on. Likewise, the ancient Greeks added an important concept to criminal law: trial by

Socrates was put to death by poison.

a jury of one's peers. Prior to the Greek *city-states*, other ancient cultures relied on kings, judges, or magicians to determine guilt or innocence. In keeping with Greek ideals of democracy, a free man who committed a crime could be judged by a group of his fellow free male citizens. (Slaves and women had no such rights.) For example, a jury of five hundred Athenians tried the famous Greek philosopher Socrates in 399 BCE. They found him guilty of "corrupting youthful minds" and believing in gods different from those of the Athenian state. Socrates was sentenced to death, thus proving that even a jury of one's peers can pass harsh and unfair sentences. Socrates was literally told, "Pick your own poison," and he chose hemlock for his execution.

Like other ancient cultures, the Greeks relied on a variety of punishments to enforce right behavior. The Greek poet Hesiod wrote in 700 BCE: "Here is the Law, as Zeus established it. . . . Justice, in the end is the . . . best thing they [humans] have." Greek philosophers emphasized that good laws should serve two functions—deterrence and rehabilitation. To this end, Greek courts punished their fellow citizens by imposing fines, loss of property, exposure to public shame, and ritual cursing. More serious crimes merited capital punishment by crucifixion, stoning, or throwing off a cliff.

Ancient Greeks also had jails, and they contributed to the development of prisons by instituting three different levels of jails (similar to today's high-, medium-, and low-security prisons) corresponding to different forms of offenses. The "low-security" Greek prisons were located near the marketplace within towns and held inmates for no longer than two years, as punishment for minor offenses. "Medium-security" prisons in ancient Greece were for those who had committed violent acts that had not been *premeditated*. These prisons were for those sentenced to more than five years of incarceration. The government assigned inmates counselors who visited them to encourage their rehabilitation before their release back into society. This concept of rehabilitation programs and counseling in prisons has also been popular at various times during the modern era. The final, extreme form of prison in ancient Greece was for those whom juries deemed incorrigible (incapable of reforming their lives). City-states built such prisons far from society, in wild, inhospitable

Crucifixion was one form of Roman execution.

places, and all inmates were held there for life. Here we see the birth of another modern concept, the life sentence. Prior to this, ancient jails and prisons were designed to hold criminals until kings or judges decided on their punishment, and violent crimes were usually punished by death. The life sentence, an invention of the ancient Greeks, is still very popular in the United States; in fact, one out of every eleven inmates in U.S. federal and state prison systems today is serving a life sentence.

ANCIENT ROME—MODERN LAW, BARBARIC TORTURES, AND THE FIRST ATTEMPTS AT PRISON REFORM

Ancient Roman justice was a study in contrasts. Ancient Rome greatly refined the science of law, and Roman laws and lawyers are the model most Western nations follow today. In fact, a modern lawyer transported in a time machine to ancient Rome could probably argue a case successfully using her modern training, as today's law practices are so dependent on ancient Rome. Although most people consider Latin a "dead language," modern lawyers use terms from ancient Rome in their everyday practice.

Ancient Roman lawyers were brilliant and efficient, but historians say they could also be barbarous in their treatment of alleged criminals. Most Roman legal punishments would certainly be termed "cruel and unusual punishment" today. The Roman state punished lesser crimes by seizing property, reducing a free person to the status of slave, public chaining, branding, whipping, forced recruitment into the army, and so on. Crimes committed against the government (any disobedience to the senate or Caesar, including political protest) were punished by savage torture and execution. Audiences of such films as *Gladiator* or *Ben Hur* understand the sorts of public tortures the ancient Roman state conducted in the name of justice. Following the slave revolt led by Spartacus, the empire crucified so many slaves that crosses bordered the Appian Way for miles. Prisoners of war, Christians, and other undesirables were covered with pitch and lit as human torches or dressed in animal skins and thrown to the lions.

At the same time, ancient Rome built a variety of different incarceration facilities. Most were short-term facilities, such as the jail cells beneath the Circus in Rome, built to hold prisoners prior to torture and execution. Ancient Rome constructed other facilities to hold citizens who

The Coliseum, in Rome, where audiences watched the executions of criminals

had gone bankrupt and owed large debts to others. Debtors' prisons held inmates for sixty days, during which friends and relatives could pay off their debts and thus secure the debtor's release. If no friends or family made such payments within the sixty days, the government then sold the debtor into slavery or executed him. Other Roman facilities were similar to the death camps of the Holocaust or the Gulag, where political prisoners performed slave labor for the state, usually resulting in death or permanent physical damage.

The savage customs of Imperial Rome led to the first known attempt at prison reform. The emperor Constantine, famous for his conversion to Christianity early in the fourth century, issued the *Theodosian Code*, the first legal document in history limiting mistreatment of prisoners. It required Imperial Roman jails to feed and bathe prison inmates and allow them to see daylight. A more radical reform came in 367 CE, when the emperor ordered all prisoners except adulterers, rapists, and murderers released from prison in honor of the Easter holiday. If enacted today, such a law would free the majority of inmates currently held in the United States!

The idea of prison reform was ancient Rome's most humane contribution to the history of punishment and incarceration. After centuries of **barbarism**, Rome ended her days with an amazingly lenient legal system. However, it was not to last long. Barbarian armies overran the empire, and civilization gave way to the Dark Ages.

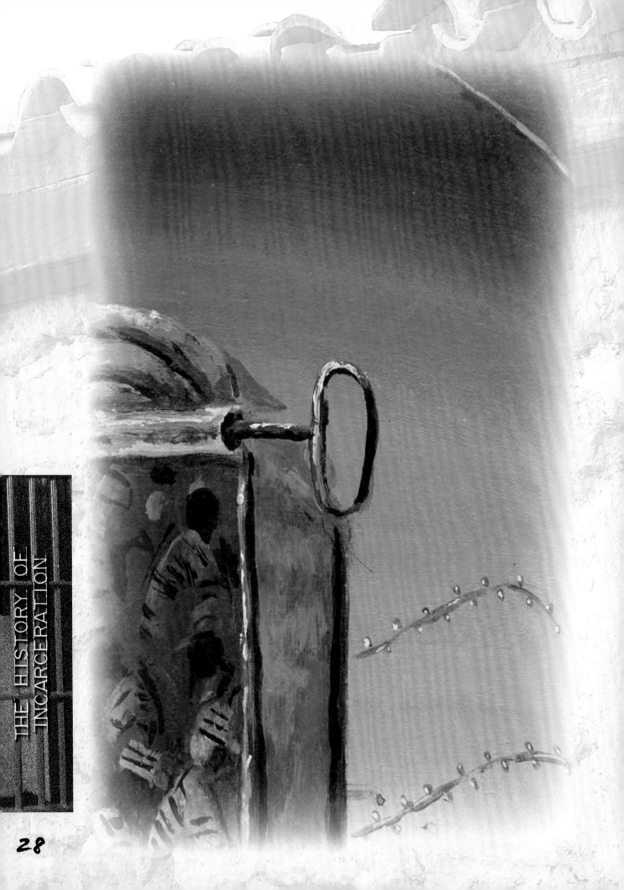

CHAPTER 2

GAOLS AND DUNGEONS: PUNISHMENT AND INCARCERATION IN MEDIEVAL TIMES

"I would rather do penance by dying than suffer any longer the agony of imprisonment." —Joan of Arc, May 28, 1431

Joan of Arc is a unique and fascinating figure in history, and the most famous inmate of medieval times. In recent years, two movies were made about her, and the popular television show *Joan of Arcadia* played off her name.

Joan of Arc was born January 6, 1412, to a pious Catholic family that named her Jeanette. When she was thirteen years old, Joan claimed to hear the voice of God in her family's garden. She said God spoke to her through Michael the Archangel, and later through saints Catherine and Margaret. The voices told her to lead the forces of her native France to war against the English, who had conquered her country. At the age of seventeen, she did so successfully, and enabled the crowning of a new French king, Charles VII.

Nowadays, women fight alongside men in most nations' armies, and some hold rank as commanders. However, in the fifteenth century, women were very limited in their social roles; men expected them to serve as wives, **concubines**, or nuns, and limit themselves to "feminine" activities like spinning, sewing, and domestic chores. It was truly a miracle that a teenage girl got herself accepted as a general and succeeded in leading a rough-and-tough band of medieval knights through a series of brutal military campaigns. Alas, though she managed the impossible, Joan was still an embarrassment to her fellow citizens, because she wore men's clothes and succeeded in men's roles. As a result, her own French leaders imprisoned her and accused her of **heresy.**

Early in her imprisonment, French authorities held Joan at the castle of Jean de Luxembourg. His wife and aunt treated Joan kindly, though they tried to persuade her to dress as a woman—a demand repeated throughout her captivity and one she consistently refused. While a prisoner at this castle, Joan attempted escape, leaping from the top of the castle's tower and falling seventy feet (21.3 meters) to the ground. Miraculously, she was unhurt; the only ill effect she suffered was an inability to eat for three days. She took this amazing risk not for her own sake but to try to save others, as she had heard the town of Compiegne was about to be attacked. Curiously, Joan said her voices told her not to jump; this is the only time she admitted disobeying what she regarded as God's command.

After this, the French handed Joan over to the English, who accused her of witchcraft and placed her in harsher confinement. English authorities imprisoned her in one of the towers of the castle of Rouen. According to the laws at the time, the English should have kept a woman

The tower where Joan of Arc was imprisoned before her execution.

accused of heresy in a church-run prison with female guards. Instead, they held Joan in a small, dark room, with the windows covered with bricks, her ankles bound, a chain fastened to a large log around her waist, and male guards watching her. The five soldiers who guarded Joan mocked her and even tried to rape her.

On May 30, 1431, authorities of the church burned Joan of Arc at the stake. Two platforms were set up in a square, one for Joan, the other for government and church officials. In the center of Joan's platform was a wooden stake, drenched with oil and sulfur. Joan listened to a sermon urging her to repent, and then she cried out, "I beg all of you standing there to forgive any harm I have done, so as I forgive you the harm you have done me, I beseech you to pray for me." As the flames consumed her flesh, Joan continually cried out the word, "Jesus!" After death, executioners threw her ashes into a river, because church law did not allow burial for convicted heretics. Twenty years later, the church ordered another trial and declared Joan innocent of all the charges they had brought against her. In 1909, the Catholic Church declared Joan to be a saint.

RELIGIOUS INCARCERATION AND PUNISHMENT

Although she was a unique individual, the imprisonment and execution of Joan of Arc shows common trends in medieval punishment. Authorities in the Middle Ages rarely used incarceration for long-term sentences. Instead, jails and dungeons held prisoners for short periods while they awaited release, ransom, torture, or execution. Medieval society did not view incarceration itself as punishment, but as a way to hold people until the church or state leaders decided what punishment would be appropriate for prisoners' crimes.

Joan also illustrates the increased importance of the Catholic Church and religious dimensions of the legal system. Historians sometimes refer to the Middle Ages as "the Age of Faith," and while religion can be a force of great good in a society, it can also be misused as a way to

control and punish people, sometimes brutally. At times, authorities in the Middle Ages punished heresy and witchcraft more brutally than murder or rape.

Medieval Europe had several different forms of religious incarceration facilities. You probably think of monasteries as places for monks to pray, work, and live holy lives—and they were. However, beginning in the 1100s, all monasteries also contained prisons. The Catholic Church in the medieval era used monastery prisons to incarcerate monks or priests for specific sentences ordered by authorities of the Church. The purpose of monastic imprisonment was rehabilitation; confinement was supposed to make the inmate a better person. The measures used to bring about rehabilitation could be harsh, however. Chains and *fetters*, restricted diets, and beatings could be part of the prison sentence. One particularly vicious monastery prison bore the ironic name *Vade in Pace* (Go in Peace).

Another medieval prison system was that of the Inquisition, the arm of the Church with the responsibility to discover, sentence, and punish

A tribunal of the Inquisition

In the sixteenth century, the Catholic Church burned William Tyndale at the stake for his crime of translating the Bible into English.

heretics. Over several hundred years, the Inquisition jailed, tortured, or executed thousands of Jews, Muslims, alleged witches, and Christians who disagreed with the Catholic Church. Joan of Arc is one of the most famous victims of the Inquisition. Inquisitors usually used imprisonment as a way to hold accused subjects while questioning and torturing them. Although the Inquisition used jails mostly for short-term incarceration,

The cage was a medieval form of imprisonment. It was hung up where passersby could observe the prisoner's suffering, and the prisoner was sometimes left there until he died.

GAOLS AND DUNGEONS

it nonetheless put a considerable strain on medieval jail facilities. The greatest number of prisoners in the Middle Ages were those accused of violating religious laws.

North Americans probably can't understand the mindset surrounding religious punishment in the Middle Ages; after all, we are accustomed to the idea of religious freedom. No such belief in religious freedom existed during medieval times. Philosophers of that age believed it was better to force a person out of their heresy—using any available means of torture or punishment—than to allow his soul to go to hell after death. As a result, the Inquisition used a number of tortures, the most common of which were burning limbs, near drowning, and stretching on "the rack," a device that slowly pulled apart the victim's muscles and bones.

SECULAR GAOLS (JAILS) AND DUNGEONS IN THE MIDDLE AGES

In England, beginning in the twelfth century, the king required each town to maintain its own jail. Some famous English prisons, including the Tower of London and Newgate Prison, date from medieval times. As with religious prisons, *secular* authorities rarely ordered lengthy terms of imprisonment. Common forms of secular punishment in the Middle Ages were public mutilation, branding, burning alive, burial alive, or decapitation. Punishment most often took the form of public spectacles, as medieval authorities relied on these to deter crime. Jails held prisoners until punishment or execution.

A common practice in medieval Europe was jailing debtors until someone (family members or friends) paid off his debts. Violent criminals were placed in the same jails as citizens whose only crime was their failure to pay someone money they owed, and this practice remained common until the nineteenth century. This is "coercive punishment"—

IT'S THE PITS

Most medieval castles included dungeons—cells for short-term captivity built in the bottom part of the fortress. The word dungeon comes from the French term *donjon*, which originally meant "tower" rather than "prison." Castle owners used the bottom parts of such towers for incarceration; hence, dungeon came to mean "castle jail." The worst castle dungeons were *oubliettes*, or "pit prisons." An oubliette was the bottom of a round tower, underground, and containing no window or even staircase for access. Captors lowered their prisoners into a pit prison by rope through a trap door. Food was lowered to the prisoners in the same way; there was no light or sanitation, and water, mud, mold, and vermin covered the floors. Such pit prisons were virtually escape proof, hellishly unsanitary, and extremely unpleasant.

captivity designed to force someone to do something (in this case pay off a debt).

Besides short-term incarceration while awaiting punishment, jails were also commonly used in the Middle Ages to confine prisoners awaiting ransom. Again, the medieval world was vastly different from our own; in this century, only terrorists hold prisoners for ransom, and doing so violates international standards for the treatment of prisoners of war. However, medieval lords and barons considered ransom to be a normal and accepted practice, and they usually held prisoners of war captive until the enemy paid for their release.

Holding prisoners for ransom was done according to the rules of **chivalry**. Prisoners awaiting ransom were of the "gentlemanly" class (knights or nobles). A knight or baron holding captives knew that in

Castle towers were some of the first prisons.

The Tower of London

future wars he might be held for ransom on the opposing side, and because of this, captives were usually treated well. They were held in aboveground rooms with adequate ventilation and furnishings. The cost of incarceration would come out of the ransom paid, so some wealthy captives received especially fine treatment.

A modern saying is that something costs "a king's ransom," meaning an outrageous amount of money. This phrase comes from the fact that more than a few kings in medieval times were captured and held for ransom. For example, when King Richard I of England, commonly known as "Richard the Lionhearted" suffered a shipwreck near Venice on his return from the **Crusades** in 1192, Duke Leopold of Austria imprisoned

GAOLS AND DUNGEONS

Newgate Prison

him. Leopold then turned King Richard over to Holy Roman Emperor Henry VI, who released him in February 1194, after English nobles paid a huge ransom.

Indeed no captive can tell his story truly, unless it be sadly.
But with an effort he can express the sadness in song.
I have many friends, but their gifts are poor.
They show me no honour, if for want of a ransom,
I am held prisoner here for two more winters.

—from a ballad written by King Richard I during his captivity

One historian described incarceration and punishment in medieval times as "a theater of horrors." Perhaps this does not surprise you, as the Dark Ages is often known for barbarism. It may be more surprising, however, to learn about incarceration and punishment in the centuries that followed the Middle Ages—what historians call the "early modern era." As we shall see, until the nineteenth century, punishments were cruel and unusual by today's standards.

CHAPTER 3

CHAOTIC JUSTICE: PUNISHMENT AND INCARCERATION IN THE SEVENTEENTH AND EIGHTEENTH CENTURIES

"The commissary of police . . . made a sign to two gendarmes, who placed themselves one on Dantes' right and the other on his left. A door that communicated with the Palais de Justice was opened, and they went through a long range of gloomy corridors, whose appearance might have made even the boldest shudder. . . . After numberless windings, Dantes saw a door with an iron wicket. The commissary took up an iron mallet and knocked thrice, every blow seeming to Dantes as if struck on his heart. The door opened, the two gendarmes gently pushed him forward, and the door closed with a loud

sound behind him. The air he inhaled was no longer pure . . . he was in prison."

—from *The Count of Monte Cristo*, by Alexandre Dumas

Perhaps you have read *The Count of Monte Cristo* or seen the action-adventure movie released in 2002, starring James Caviezel. The film and the novel on which it is based are about Edmond Dantes, an innocent man wrongfully imprisoned in the Chateau d'If, an island prison just off the coast of the French city of Marseille. The Chateau d'If is sometimes called "the French Alcatraz" because, like its modern American counterpart, it is a vast, seemingly ***impregnable*** island prison fortress. Dantes spends fourteen years in this gloomy incarceration facility, all the time plotting his escape, as well as his revenge on the man who put him there.

While imprisoned in the Chateau d'If, Dantes hears a neighboring prisoner digging a tunnel, so he begins digging toward this fellow inmate. When the tunnel to other prisoner's cell is completed, this fellow captive turns out to be a learned man, who teaches Dantes languages, science, sword fighting, and other subjects necessary for the education of a gentleman. The two inmates become as close as father and son, so when Dantes' companion is about to die, he reveals the hidden location of a fabulous buried treasure. His friend's death enables Dantes to make a daring escape, wrapped in a burial shroud, impersonating the corpse. Guards toss Dantes over the cliffs of the island into the ocean, and he swims to freedom. This amazing escape is only the beginning of Dantes' adventures, as he assumes a new identity as the wealthy and mysterious Count of Monte Cristo.

The Count of Monte Cristo is pure fiction, but the Chateau d'If is a real place with a long and somber history. King Francois I laid down its first stone in 1516, and the fortress was finished in 1529. Beginning in 1634, the rulers of France used the chateau for political prisoners. One of these was Joseph Custoldi de Faria, a hypnotist, ***spiritualist***, and sailor who may have inspired Dumas' character, Edmond Dantes. Today, the Chateau d'If is a tourist site. If you visit Marseille, France, you can pay a guide to take you by boat to the island, where you can pretend to be Edmond

THE HISTORY OF INCARCERATION

The Chateau d'If today

Dantes plotting his escape from the dire prison fortress. The Chateau d'If is part of the fascinating history of penology in the early modern era.

PUBLIC DISGRACE AND EXECUTIONS

As in previous generations, public spectacles to shame or execute criminals were the main method of enforcing laws in Europe and its colonies in the 1600s and 1700s. Prisons became more common, but these were for debtors more than for criminals, and the conditions of these prisons differed greatly from one another, depending on who was in charge. The Chateau d'If, a large and efficiently managed prison, was unusual at this time. Overall, the administration of justice was chaotic and unpredictable in this era.

CHAOTIC JUSTICE

45

Hester Pryne was forced to wear a scarlet letter to tell everyone she met of her crime.

You may have read Nathaniel Hawthorne's famous novel, *The Scarlet Letter*, which is set in Puritan New England during the 1600s. The main character, Hester Prynne, is a young woman whose husband is far away when she becomes pregnant, so it is obvious she has committed adultery—a terrible sin in this very religious community. Hester will not reveal her sexual partner (he happens to be the local minister), so as punishment, the town elders force her to wear a large letter "A" (for adulterer) over her chest whenever she is in public. The authorities intend this punishment to both shame her and help her **repent**.

Hester Prynne is a fictional character, but the punishment she receives is authentic. In Europe and in the American colonies in the seventeenth and eighteenth centuries, a broad variety of punishments took their power from community shame. Wearing letters or special clothing or standing in the village square and confessing one's crime to the town were milder forms of public humiliation. Whipping or branding were more serious forms of public correction. In the colony of Maryland, for example, in the mid-seventeenth century, authorities punished anyone speaking disrespectfully of the English king or the Virgin Mary by public whipping. Branding was similar to the "scarlet letter" form of punishment, but officials burned brands in prominent places on the criminal's body in order to serve as a permanent source of public shame.

If you have visited a reconstructed colonial community such as Colonial Williamsburg in Virginia, you may have seen a "pillory." Common in Europe and the English colonies of the 1700s, the pillory was a board atop a post. The condemned criminal would stand upright, his head and hands locked in the board. Persons locked in the pillory were subjects of public **derision**, exposed not only to the terrible discomfort of standing upright for long hours, unable to relieve themselves privately, but also to spitting or objects thrown at them by the public. Depending on the length of the sentence, the pillory could inflict a short time of public humiliation, physical discomfort, serious crippling, or even death.

Another serious form of public punishment during this time was mutilation. The most common form was cutting off hands for thievery, cuts on the cheek for violent offenders, and amputation of thumbs for those

Sarah Good was hung as a witch in Salem, Massachusetts.

who committed business fraud. Other forms of mutilation were cutting off an ear and, less frequently, blinding.

WITCH HUNTS

"You're a liar! I'm no more a witch than you are a wizard!"
—Sarah Good, about to be hanged as a witch in Salem, Massachusetts, July 19, 1692, responding to the minister's request that she confess her sin of witchcraft

As in the Middle Ages, church and state authorities in the seventeenth century sometimes punished harshly those who disagreed with their religious beliefs. The most infamous case of religious punishment in the English colonies is the "witch trials" held in Salem, Massachusetts, from 1692 until 1693. There is no proof that anyone accused actually believed in or practiced witchcraft, but nineteen people were accused, convicted, and executed as witches during this time.

The Salem witch trials, awful as they were, were mild compared to earlier ones in Europe. Gruesome punishment of witches was especially common in France and Germany, and *The Malleus Maleficarum* was a popular guidebook on how to find and kill witches. In the late Middle Ages and early modern age, European authorities developed dozens of torture tools and methods especially for accused witches. One torture device, called bootikens, was a boot extending from the victim's ankles to knees. Witch-hunters hammered wedges up the boot into the victim's leg, crushing bones. Torturers inserted another tool, the pear, into the body cavities of alleged witches and then expanded the device until it tore the victim apart from the inside out. Yet another torture device, the turcas, tore out witches' fingernails. Authorities also subjected alleged witches to drowning, stoning, and crushing with heavy weights. It is ironic that these hellish methods of torture were supposed to rid society of evil, when it is obvious that the true evil was being carried out by those members of society who tortured innocents, mostly older women, for imaginary sorceries.

Sometimes, people do learn from the past. When the thirteen English colonies in the New World achieved independence from the crown, they adopted a set of amendments to the Constitution of the newly formed United States. The first of these declared that government could not prohibit the free exercise of religion. Citizens of the United States had learned from the terrible mistakes of their Puritan ancestors how governments could misuse religious laws, and thus, they formed a new kind of government that allowed religious freedom, a successful experiment that has spread to most nations in the world today.

THE DEATH PENALTY

Execution was common punishment for all sorts of crimes in the seventeenth and eighteenth centuries. Authorities ordered the death penalty not as much for the serious nature of crimes as for repeated crimes. Correction in early modern Europe and the colonies depended on actions of public shame, designed to keep criminals from repeating actions, and society relied on such public humiliation to rehabilitate wrongdoers. A first-time lawbreaker usually received a light sentence, such as a short time in the pillory. If he committed a second crime, the judge ordered a stiffer sentence, such as branding or mutilation. If a criminal committed yet another crime, the judge sentenced him to public execution.

Public officials conducted executions with great ceremony. They were theatrical events designed to teach the public a lesson, and the lesson was, "Don't even think of committing a crime such as this!" Forms of execution included beheading, strangling, the firing squad, and burial while alive, but hangings were most common. Before execution, an official read the death sentence aloud to the criminal, along with a detailed recounting of the crimes, and a priest or minister delivered a sermon urging the condemned man to express sadness over his crime and ask forgiveness from God and the public. Supposedly, these actions allowed the convict to unburden his soul and find his way to heaven in the afterlife. At the same time, authorities staged executions to impress on the

At one time, hangings were a common form of capital punishment in America.

audience how the government would punish such crimes, deterring similar actions in the future.

Today, the death penalty is controversial. Many modern nations such as Canada have banned the practice, though the United States still executes offenders. However, in the 1700s and 1800s, citizens of most nations throughout the word viewed capital punishment as necessary for recidivists (persons who repeatedly committed crimes). Only a single religious group, the Quakers, objected to the practice.

BANISHMENT

If authorities were merciful, or if they were simply too busy to stage a public execution, Europeans and colonial rulers used another form of punishment, banishment. In the colonies, this took a very simple form— "Leave this town and never return, or face death if you do." The Bible story of Cain, whom God banished for killing his brother Abel, provided a religious justification for such treatment. Town leaders often forced families of criminals to suffer banishment along with them.

In remote frontier areas, banished convicts had to survive alone in the wilderness or move in with Native peoples. In more settled areas, criminals could move into other towns and start life anew. This was not always easy, however, as many towns and villages in the colonial era demanded that new settlers provide letters of reference before they could move into the community.

Today, banishment is seldom practiced; it seems ineffective because it merely transfers problems from one location to another. In the early modern era, there was less communication between villages, and less concern for the welfare of the state or country as opposed to the welfare of a particular community. Removing undesired citizens was a simple and inexpensive way to protect a community from crime.

In Europe and England, banishment to the colonies was common. Authorities shackled prisoners convicted of serious crimes and put them aboard vessels headed to the Americas or Australia. There was little sense of global community in the 1600s and 1700s, and citizens of the "Old World" cared little how their colonies fared as long as violent criminals were out of sight and out of mind. At the same time, banishment allowed the banished to begin life anew and many thus punished did live reformed lives.

A social worker from a major city recently told the story of a police force that had a common off-the-record practice for dealing with minor crimes. Instead of arresting individuals for disturbing the peace or disorderly conduct, police officers simply gave the offenders enough money for a bus ticket and encouraged them to take up residence in another city. The problem was then off their streets! (Although, unfortunately, the problem no doubt continued to exist somewhere else.)

PRISONS IN THE EARLY MODERN ERA

The 1700s and 1800s saw an expansion of jails and prisons, but not for the reasons authorities use them today. Many of the jails in early modern Europe and England contained debtors and people in poverty. Governments designed these workhouses to hold people who owed money to others or were too poor to support themselves. Such institutions were more akin to slave camps or sweatshops than to modern incarceration facilities.

Inmates often lived in these facilities with their families, and sometimes even their extended families. Conditions varied considerably, depending on the jail keeper and local community standards. In some facilities, inmates were allowed to drink alcohol, gamble, and receive visitors

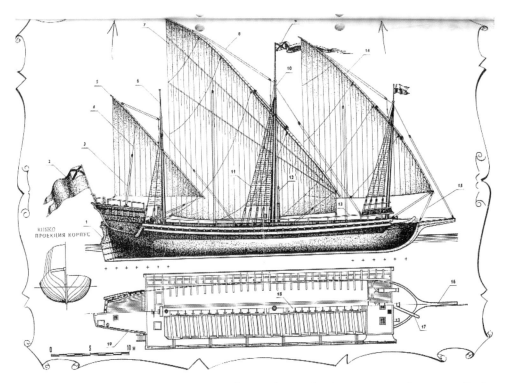

Galley ships depended on rowers as well as sails—and prisoners sometimes supplied the power.

from the outside whenever they wished; other facilities were stricter, requiring prisoners to work long hours and prohibiting leisure. If prisoners and their families had friends or relatives who provided goods and services for them, they would live in better conditions than those who lacked such resources.

Prison keepers were business people, rather than government officials, who ran their penal facilities as an investment, profiting from the work of their inmates. Governments allowed each prison keeper to make rules and regulations for his own facility. Protection, food, medical care, and other important considerations depended entirely on the individual prison keeper. Some facilities housed violent criminals alongside debtors and victims of poverty.

"WE KEEP YOU ALIVE TO SERVE THIS SHIP"

For the worst violent criminals, seventeenth-century European nations had a particularly harsh form of imprisonment—the galleys. Although sails were common, warships continued to rely on rowers for movement in battle. Thus, as in ancient Roman times, the worst criminals were sentenced to short and brutal lives pulling at the oars below decks.

Toward the end of the seventeenth century, the Dutch began a new type of penal institution called the *beterhuis*. These prisons held only criminals (rather than debtors or the poor) in individual cells, with their eventual rehabilitation the goal. The beterhuis was the world's first glimpse at what lay ahead; it was the ancestor of modern penal systems.

CHAPTER 4

THE FIRST PENITENTIARIES: ENGLAND AND NORTH AMERICA CREATE THE MODERN PRISON SYSTEM, 1780–1900

"Everything passes in the most profound silence, and nothing is heard in the whole prison but the steps of those who march. . . . The silence within these vast walls was that of death . . . there were a thousand living beings, and yet it was a desert solitude."

—two French visitors describing their experience visiting the prison in Auburn, New York, in 1831

The French visitors were astonished seeing the incredible efficiency of the prison at Auburn, where guards quickly punished inmates for speaking to one another, and the whole complex operated like a vast soundless machine. American prisons of the early nineteenth century were especially impressive considering how they contrasted with prisons only half a century before that time. Throughout the eighteenth century, detention centers were anything but quiet and orderly. In Europe and North America, prisons were utterly chaotic. Governments allowed jail and workhouse administrators to do anything they pleased with their inmates. In many prisons during the 1700s, jail keepers permitted inmates to make up their own rules and live as they pleased. Some incarceration facilities were like slave labor camps, where inmates worked without stopping; others allowed inmates to spend their days drinking and gambling. There was no rhyme, reason, or order to prisons in the 1700s. Yet a century later, authorities ran prisons in the United States and England like clockwork, everything controlled by detailed rules and regulations.

The end of the eighteenth century saw the beginnings of modern prisons. Barred cells; prisoners marched from place to place by guards; the grey, bare sameness of rooms and hallways: all these things came into existence at the turn of the century. While some critics would say the system was cruel and ineffective, it came into being through the good intentions of persons who hoped to improve prisons and rehabilitate prisoners.

PRISON-SYSTEM REFORMERS

The modern jail system came about in large part from the influence of Quakers, a *pacifist* religious group. Founded in England by George Fox (1624–1691), the Society of Friends, informally known as Quakers, were devout Christians who believed a part of God's nature lived within every person; therefore, they refused to kill other people. A group of Friends led by William Penn settled the English colony of Pennsylvania (named after their founder) in the late 1600s.

William Penn

The Quakers had faced legal persecution in England, so they sympathized with criminals who were mistreated in the colonies.

The Quakers were sickened by the ways society tortured, shamed, and executed criminals; such behavior went against their spiritual beliefs. In 1682, the Quaker rulers of Pennsylvania passed what they called "the Great Law." This included the rule that the colony of Pennsylvania must punish crimes by confinement in a "house of correction" rather than by public humiliation, torment, or execution. This was a major turning point in the history of criminal punishment. For thousands of years, in most nations of the world, rulers had assumed prison was a temporary measure to hold accused persons until they could "properly" punish them in some other way. The Quakers believed it was inhumane to humiliate, torture, or kill offenders; they felt incarceration was a more compassionate alternative.

The royal English government feared Pennsylvania's law code would create lawlessness in the American colonies, so in 1718, England forced Pennsylvania to go back to "normal" means of criminal punishment (public humiliation, torture, and execution). However, as soon as the American colonies obtained freedom from English rule, the new state of Pennsylvania changed back to their Quaker way of doing things. In 1790, Dr. Benjamin Rush, one of the signers of the Declaration of Independence, signed a law that required Pennsylvania to punish convicted criminals by imprisonment. This law was a key part of the Pennsylvania prison system, which would soon influence prisons around the world.

At the same time, in England, John Howard pushed for reform of English jails. A religious-minded country gentleman and sheriff of Bedfordshire, Howard officially had authority over the local jail. Unlike almost all other sheriffs of his time, Howard decided to actually visit a jail and talk with the inmates. He was shocked by living conditions there, which he believed were the opposite of those required by "Christian charity."

His curiosity and anger aroused, Howard went around England and Wales investigating conditions in other incarceration facilities. He saw filthy and disorderly jails and prison hulks—ships anchored off the shore of British cities that held prisoners in dark, diseased, and smelly spaces beneath their decks. After his investigation, Howard published a book in 1777 titled *The State of the Prisons of England and Wales*, a publication that called for reforming jails and prisons on the British Isles. Howard continued his crusade for prison reform, traveling throughout Europe and often visiting dangerous and unhealthy facilities until 1791, when he died visiting a Russian prison.

Like the Quakers in Pennsylvania, Howard believed incarceration was a more civilized approach to punishment than the public torments common in his day. However, he did not believe that jails and prisons as they existed in his time could help inmates. They were unhealthy and

disorderly, serving only to make prisoners sicker, both physically and morally. Howard argued prisons must be orderly, both to prevent physical diseases and to make inmates better people. Howard and political allies succeeded in making Parliament pass a bill in 1779 to establish "penitentiary houses," where prisoners would be kept in clean, separate cells. Local governors often ignored the bill, but its passage helped lead to the era of modern prisons.

Note John Howard's use of the word "penitentiary." That word contains a philosophy important over the next two centuries. Howard and the Pennsylvania Quakers assumed people committed crimes because of their *environment*, an idea often **espoused** by parents when they tell their children, "Don't hang around with the wrong crowd or they'll influence you to get into trouble." Religious *idealists* of the late 1700s believed the cure for bad social influence was solitude (isolation from other people). If society kept a criminal away from bad influences, the inmate would then become penitent (sorry for his sins). Thus, the penitentiary was a facility where inmates were isolated from society and from one another due to the belief that such isolation would lead to sorrow over crime. These beliefs played an important role in founding the modern prison system.

THE FIRST PENITENTIARIES

"Let the avenue to this house be rendered difficult and gloomy by mountains and morasses. Let the doors be of iron, and let the grating, occasioned by opening and shutting them, be increased by an echo that shall deeply pierce the soul."
—Dr. Benjamin Rush, Quaker reformer, 1787

Reformers were anxious to see their ideas for a prison that would make criminals penitent put into practice. According to historians, Philadelphia's Walnut Street Jail, built in 1790, was "the first true correctional institution in America." Unlike workhouses and jails of the time, the

The use of stocks was common practice in workhouses.

Walnut Street Jail housed only convicted criminals. In keeping with the theories of Howard and the Quakers, wardens kept inmates separate from one another in order to have plenty of quiet time to reconsider their way of life. Other new prisons soon copied the Walnut Street Jail on a larger scale. Examples were the Newgate, New York, prison of 1797; the State Prison at Charlestown, Massachusetts, established in 1805; and Maryland State Penitentiary, which opened in 1811. These were the first of the "Big Houses," where incarceration was practiced on a large scale.

Two penitentiaries built in the first quarter of the nineteenth century became famous and had worldwide influence. One was the Auburn, New York, prison begun in 1816. Architects designed this facility so prisoners lived and ate together but received punishment for talking with one another. The Auburn prison became the model for more than thirty state prisons, the most famous being Sing Sing prison in Ossining, New York, built in 1825.

The most important prison in history, however, was Eastern State Penitentiary, constructed in Philadelphia, Pennsylvania, in 1829. Eastern State Penitentiary was built on the "solitary" model of prison design, where each inmate was kept in a cell and not allowed to see the face of any fellow prisoner. More than three hundred jails and prisons around the world copied the building design and practices of Eastern Penitentiary, and in many ways, it served as the model for today's prison system.

LIFE AT EASTERN STATE

"I know being punished is unpleasant, but it hurts me more than it hurts you."
—an anonymous parent

Have you ever heard your parents say the above statement? You may have responded, "Yeah, right!" Well, the religious prison reformers of the early 1800s claimed they were building these new prisons to help reform criminals, and by all accounts, they were also sincere in their good intentions. Despite this, the experience of life at Eastern State Penitentiary was simply awful.

The moment an inmate entered the Penitentiary, a guard placed a hood over his head so other prisoners would not see him. During the entire time of incarceration, he would not see the face of another inmate. The guard did not allow him to socialize, read a newspaper, play ball, have visits from friends, receive letters from the outside world, or do

DOES YOUR SCHOOL EVER FEEL LIKE JAIL? (THERE MAY BE A REASON FOR THAT!)

Nowadays, prisons are mostly "out of sight, out of mind." However, a century and a half ago, the public was crazy about the new penitentiary system. Supporters said this "social experiment" could transform not only prisoners but also the entire nation. They believed the combination of strict discipline, order, and time alone for reflection could become "a remedy for all the evils of society." Reformers of the time suggested that prison discipline should serve as a model for other social institutions—such as schools. As one prison chaplain insisted, if everyone in society could spend a few years in a prison-like environment, "the world would ultimately be the better for it." Sitting bored and silent in study hall, you may disagree with him.

anything else—except read the Bible and work. The only entertainment was the preaching of ministers, who stood outside prisoners' cells delivering sermons, and an hour-long "outing" each day alone that enabled the prisoner to move around in the fresh air of the small courtyard.

Quakers did not allow guards to whip inmates at Eastern State Penitentiary, but they used other types of *corporal punishment*. Prisoners who attempted to communicate with fellow inmates were denied food or blankets. Guards treated serious violations more harshly. They kept one prisoner in a dark cell in irons for forty-two days, and when a counselor discovered the delirious inmate and gave him some bread and water, administrators fired the counselor. Another punishment used at Eastern State was the "shower bath," in which guards stripped an inmate,

Eastern State Penitentiary is closed, but its gloomy walls still stand.

chained him to an outside wall, and repeatedly doused him with cold water (which sometimes formed ice on the inmate's body). The "iron gag," a five-inch (12.7-centimeter) piece of metal that fit over the inmate's tongue, was even crueler. The iron gag was chained to the inmate's wrist, and at least one inmate died from this form of punishment.

CONTROVERSY OVER EASTERN STATE PENITENTIARY

Eastern State Penitentiary was amazingly popular as a tourist site and model for correctional facilities around the world. Costing more than $700,000, it was the most expensive building in the United States when built. More than ten thousand tourists a year came to see the building, and officials celebrated the "solitary confinement" model as the way of the future, turning **uncouth** criminals into reformed citizens.

While religious reformers, politicians, and philosophers sang the praises of the Eastern State Penitentiary reform model, critics questioned whether the new prison really did inmates any good. Charles Dickens visited Eastern State Penitentiary in 1842 and later wrote:

> The System is rigid, strict and hopeless . . . and I believe it to be cruel and wrong. . . . I hold this slow and daily tampering with the mysteries of the brain, to be immeasurably worse than any torture of the body.

The *London Times* newspaper claimed Eastern State Penitentiary was "maniac-making." Not surprisingly, wardens of the penitentiary denied their system made anyone crazy. While they admitted numerous inmates did develop psychological problems, they claimed these illnesses were the results of "excessive masturbation," and hence the prisoners' own fault, rather than that of the prison. Eventually, charges of psychological damage caused Pennsylvania to ease the rules at Eastern State Penitentiary, discarding the black hoods and cruel punishments and allowing communication between prisoners.

A cell in Eastern State Penitentiary

Writer Mike Walsh, in an online article titled *Black Hoods and Iron Gags*, presents a moving account of how incarceration at Eastern State Penitentiary influenced inmates:

> The loneliness and tedium envelopes you in dread. . . . Here you are hardly human, just a number in a solitary cell. You have nightmares about the iron gag, the black hood, and water freezing your eyes, ears, and nostrils. You learn to believe in God and you pray to Him for salvation because otherwise you will go nuts. . . . And when you have finished giving up a chunk of your life, you will be cleansed and reformed, and you will go forth sinning no more because you never, ever want to be led into that giant stone house on the hill again, the place where it took every ounce of strength to keep from going stark raving mad.

RUTHLESS EFFICIENCY BECOMES THE PRISON STANDARD IN THE ENGLISH-SPEAKING WORLD

By the middle 1800s, U.S. model prisons had influenced the construction and running of penal facilities throughout Britain, Canada, and the United States. Although little solid proof supported the view that these "Big Houses" produced genuine reform in criminals, authorities worldwide viewed them as patterns for other correctional units.

Canadian authorities designed Kingston Penitentiary on the Pennsylvania pattern. Guards there made sure inmates kept "unbroken silence" between one another, not exchanging even "winks, looks, nods, or laughs." They also made sure inmates kept "perfect obedience and submission to their keepers." Guards treated harshly those who failed to obey them; in 1845, guards whipped a ten-year-old inmate at Kingston Penitentiary fifty-seven times for "staring, winking, and laughing."

The Pennsylvania system inspired a number of prisons in England during the latter half of the nineteenth century, and the English even outdid the U.S. model in strictness and efficiency. British prisons in the *Victorian Era* emphasized "hard labor," and that did not just mean working hard—it meant physical suffering and emotional pain, given in carefully measured scientific doses. For example, authorities commonly forced prisoners to do 8,640 daily steps on the "treadwheel." Do not think this was like the exercise machine with a similar name at your local health club; the treadwheel was for torture, not fitness. Rough-and-tough male inmates sometimes broke down crying from the pain of this daily routine.

English Victorian prisons also developed special diets, determined to make incarceration as cruel as possible. Scientists decided how much was the very least an inmate could eat and not starve to death, then other scientists developed ways to process food so it would feel, taste, and smell

Prison cells were tiny cubicles.

bad. Some prisoners suffered from malnutrition because they could not digest this specially designed, foul food.

In the United States, Canada, and England, jails were designed like cattle pens, so inmates could be moved from cell to work or to other units without seeing or talking to fellow inmates. Prison architects created special assembly rooms with tiny pens in which each prisoner stood without seeing fellow inmates, yet remained visible to the guards. They designed women's prisons with tiny cubicles where women sat knitting under the watchful eyes of guards, yet they were unable to see or converse with one another. Following the Pennsylvania model and taking it to extremes, prisons became more and more machine-like, **dehumanizing**, and ruthlessly efficient.

For almost a century, prisons in the English-speaking world attempted to follow the Pennsylvania penitentiary model of isolation that would supposedly reform inmates. It was an idea begun by spiritually minded idealists, but it often wound up as an excuse for **sadistic** guards and wardens to torture their prisoners. Although created to improve lives, it produced numerous cases of insanity. The penitentiary system did replace public humiliation, torture, and execution, and some historians argue it was more humane than these previous practices. Eventually, however, even the most enthusiastic supporters of the system had to admit it failed to achieve the hoped-for reform of criminals. At the start of the twentieth century, officials in the United States, Canada, and Great Britain acknowledged that the system was broken.

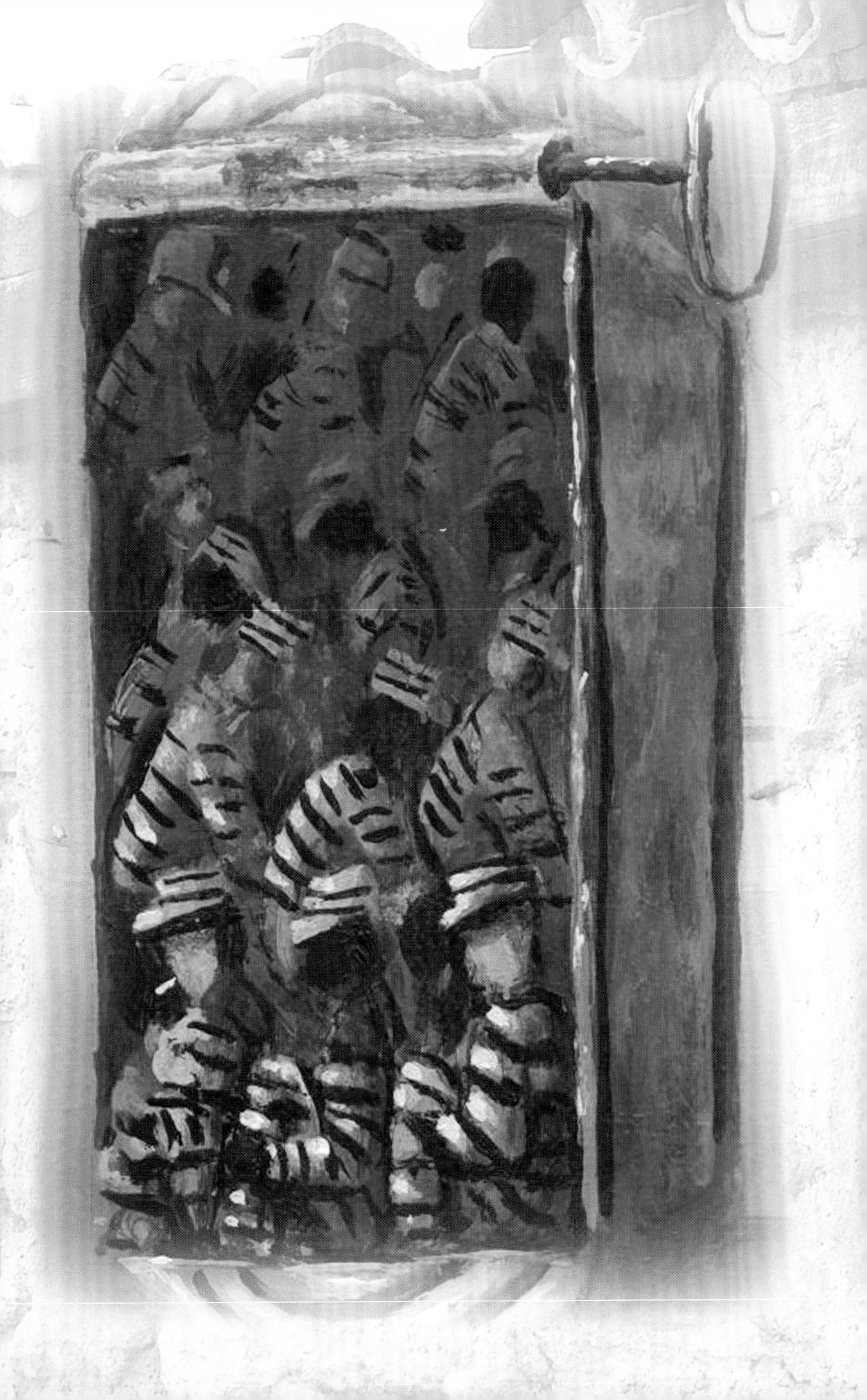

CHAPTER 5

REFORMS AND FAILURES: STRUGGLES WITHIN PRISON SYSTEMS, 1900–2000

It takes a worried man to sing a worried song,
It takes a worried man to sing a worried song,
I'm worried now, but I won't be worried long.

I went across the river, and I lay down to sleep,
I went across the river, and I lay down to sleep,
When I woke up with the shackles on my feet.

Twenty-nine links of chain around my leg,
Twenty-nine links of chain around my leg,
And on each link is initial of my name.

I asked the judge what might be my fine,
I asked the judge what might be my fine,
"Twenty-one years on the Rocky Mountain line."

The train arrived, sixteen coaches long,
The train arrived, sixteen coaches long,
The girl I love is on that train and gone.

If any one asks you who composed this song,
If any one asks you who composed this song,
Tell him it was I and I sing it all day long.

—"Worried Man Blues," a traditional folk song

A MOVIE FANTASY OF THE GREAT DEPRESSION ERA

You may have seen the movie *O Brother, Where Art Thou?* (a folk musical released in the year 2000). The film begins with a chain gang, clad in prisoners' black-and-white striped uniforms, singing and swinging their pickaxes in unison. The camera then shifts to three convicts who have obviously escaped from the chain gang. Everett (George Clooney), Pete (John Turturro), and Delmar (Tim Blake Nelson) run and hide from the chain gang and try to jump into a boxcar on a moving train. Getting aboard the moving train is especially difficult because the three are still chained together. If one slips, all three will miss the train. They manage to clamber aboard the train car and find it filled with hoboes, a common occurrence during the **Great Depression** era of history. Though the film is a fun fantasy, the setting reflects actual penal history—history still relevant today.

Many men were on the road during the Great Depression. The lack of jobs led to a sense of despair and desperation that sometimes made men turn to crime.

Today's prison system has its roots in history.

BEEVILLE, TEXAS, 2003

Inmates pound the ground to clear a space for crops, a process called flat weeding. Guards armed with .357 magnum pistols and authorized to kill watch them warily. One of the guards sits apart on horseback, armed with a 30/30 rifle capable of bringing down a fleeing convict at long range. As they work in the hot sun, the chain gang sings songs that date back generations. Prisoners portrayed in *O Brother, Where Art Thou?* sang some of these songs. A number of the songs go back to the days of slavery in the Deep South, a fact made more meaningful because over half of these twenty-first century chain gang workers are black. As Anna Mundow points out in an article for *Diversity News,* the chain gang is not an artifact of the past, but a reality of today's incarceration system with its roots in a history almost a century old.

An early chain gang

Throughout the twentieth century, prison officials struggled with problems of growing prison populations and frustration at the failures of various systems that were supposed to rehabilitate inmates. Especially in the United States, prison populations grew, and the public had to find the means to pay for expanded correctional facilities. In the South, facilities leased inmates to private contractors to perform hard labor on chain gangs. This system was controversial, as guards shot and killed scores of inmates who attempted to escape. Chain gangs remain controversial; some see them as virtual slave labor, while others argue the gangs are popular with inmates as a way to get fresh air and a change of scenery

REFORMS AND FAILURES

One of the South's chain gangs

while performing tasks useful for the larger community. Chain gangs are just one part of the continuing struggle to refine the practice of incarceration.

SLAVERY ENDS AND PRISON LABOR BEGINS IN THE AMERICAN SOUTH

In the previous chapter, we saw how religious idealists developed the penitentiary system and put it into practice, and then hundreds of prisons around the world copied the model. This system assumed complete isolation and strict discipline would make prisoners "penitent" for their crimes and return them to society reformed.

After decades of high hopes, even the strongest supporters of the penitentiary system finally had to admit failure; their "model" prisons did not eliminate crime or make criminals better citizens. Some blamed the failure on the idea itself; they argued that years of utter isolation could only make people crazy. Others blamed failure on the difference between the ideal and the reality of prison life. As the population confined to correctional facilities swelled and incarceration cost the public more money, prisoners were jammed together into cells designed for only one person, heating and cooling systems failed to operate properly, guards were often more abusive than corrective, and, in general, the best laid plans of prison designers failed to turn out anything like the way they had intended. By the time the U.S. Civil War ended, prison operators were looking for a new direction. One direction they chose was prison labor.

In 2003, 44 percent of state and federal inmates were black, compared with 35 percent white, 19 percent Latino, and 2 percent other races. Why are blacks incarcerated so much more than people of other races? In his book *Worse Than Slavery*, historian David Oshinsky claims America's tendency to incarcerate blacks goes back to the end of the Civil War and

the abolition of slavery. In 1865, the South needed to rebuild its economy. Institutions like Mississippi's Parchman Farm changed from slave plantations into prisons in order to make money for a state that had lost huge amounts of income from the loss of slave labor.

In order to incarcerate large numbers of blacks, Southern lawmakers created "Black Codes," which listed specific crimes for blacks, such as "mischief" and "insulting gestures." Prison business owners paid judges to convict blacks for slight or imaginary reasons and send them to prison. Soon, Southern jails "turned black." Private owners, many of them former slave masters, paid for prison laborers, who worked for nothing doing hard labor. As Ryan Haywood put it in his article "The Color of Justice" for the *Black Commentator,* "Mass incarceration became the 'cash crop' of the South."

Prisoners doing road work in North Carolina in the early twentieth century.

Slaves provided the labor on Southern plantations—but with the end of slavery, prisoners began to supply the South's labor needs.

Prison laborers helped build a variety of products, including ships.

THE ACA—SEEKING TO IMPROVE THE JUSTICE SYSTEM INTERNATIONALLY FOR 135 YEARS

The ideas of Maconochie and Crofton became popular in Europe and the United States and attracted the attention of prison-reform zealot Enoch Wines. Wines believed prison reform required the attention of an international organization, so in 1870, he began the National Prison Congress with members from Canada, the United States, and South America. The first president of the National Prison Congress was Rutherford B. Hayes, who later became president of the United States. The National Prison Congress eventually changed its name to the American Prison Association, and then more recently became the American Correctional Association (ACA). The ACA still functions as "a professional organization for all professionals and groups, both public and private that share a common goal of improving the justice system."

In the early 1900s, while prisons in the South of the United States continued to be characterized by chain gangs, prisons in the North entered the so-called "industrial period." These incarceration facilities commonly contained factories and produced a broad range of products for the government, the public, and the military. This trend, which continues today, was in part due to a new philosophy—the prison as "reformatory."

The reformatory in Mansfield, Ohio, in 1886

REFORMATORY TRENDS IN INCARCERATION

In the late 1800s, the ghost-like quiet and machine-like efficiency of prisons in the United States and other English-speaking nations broke down, partly due to the inhumanity and ineffectiveness of the penitentiary approach, and partly due to the difficulty and expense of running such systems. Captain Alexander Maconochie, a Scotsman living in Australia, and Sir Walter Crofton, an Irishman, together laid the foundations for a new approach—the reformatory system. Like the penitentiary system, this model was designed to rehabilitate prisoners rather than merely punish

The Kansas State Reformatory

them, but it was based on very different theories. In Australia, Maconochie introduced what he called the "mark system," which replaced the previous concept of a definite prison sentence. The mark system was similar to some methods of parenting, where parents allow children in a family greater freedom and rewards for completing chores and exhibiting good behavior. Under the mark system, prisoners "worked off" their sentence by completing work and by good behavior. According to Maconochie's theory, this gave prisoners reason to reform themselves.

In Ireland, Sir Walter Crofton added a new component to this reform model of prisoner release—probation. As a further incentive to reform (and stay reformed), government authorities kept in touch with prisoners for a time after their release to see if they could live within set guidelines of appropriate behavior for free citizens. Breaking parole resulted in

return to prison. U.S. and Canadian justice systems today largely follow Crofton's model of probation after release from jail or prison.

The Elmira Reformatory, which opened in 1876 in Elmira, New York, became the world's new model prison. Its founder, Zebulon Brockway, created it as a way to demonstrate how the new models of prison reform would work in practice. New York sentenced first-time offenders between sixteen and thirty years of age to Elmira Reformatory. Like former penitentiaries, inmates stayed in private cells; however, they worked together during the day. Unlike the previous system, inmates received extensive training for trades and educational opportunities. They worked in a number of different industries to learn new skills and provide income for the reformatory. Between 1876 and 1913, Elmira Reformatory served as the model for at least seventeen new institutions.

The reformatory model established at Elmira did prove effective, at least at first. The emphasis on reduced sentences for good behavior and improving inmates' education did rehabilitate convicted criminals. However, the Elmira Reformatory was expensive to maintain. Over the years, governments were unable to keep paying good teachers, counselors, and guards needed to reform inmates. As cheaper, poorly trained workers became common, the reformatories ceased to be effective. This struggle between the desire to rehabilitate inmates and the lack of money needed to do so has been a continuing pattern in justice systems for the past century. However, the reformatory model did create many factories in prisons and helped begin the large-scale, prison-labor system that still dominates U.S. prisons today.

EUROPE MOVES AWAY FROM PRISONS

While English-speaking nations were attempting to reform incarcerated prisoners, parts of Europe were moving away from prisons altogether. In the late nineteenth century, citizens of France, Belgium, and Sweden became concerned with developments within their prisons. Inmates

Castles were often the earliest forms of European prisons.

were developing their own prison culture, forming gangs, tattooing themselves, using special prison expressions in their speech, and even raping one another. These are all common behaviors in U.S. prisons today, but reform-minded Europeans were aghast at these developments and were concerned that prisons were causing first-time inmates to become more criminal in behavior, rather than reformed. Because of such concerns, European governments worked to develop alternatives to incarceration.

REFORMS AND FAILURES

Between 1888 and 1918, France, Belgium, Luxembourg, Portugal, Norway, Italy, Bulgaria, Denmark, Sweden, Spain, Hungary, Greece, the Netherlands, and Finland all used the "suspended sentence." Authorities told first-time criminal offenders what their sentence would be, and then told them that they would be free from this sentence as long as they did not commit any further crimes. At the same time, European authorities paroled many incarcerated criminals before completion of their sentences. Another alternative to incarceration was "patronage"—a practice in which authorities placed a first-time offender under the authority of another citizen, who was responsible to monitor the offender's behavior and help with their social education.

All these alternatives to incarceration proved effective in Europe. Between 1887 and 1956, the percentage of incarcerated citizens dropped by more than 50 percent in France. Most European countries lowered their percentage of incarcerated population during this time. Exceptions were Germany, Italy, and Russia, which in the early 1900s were heading for the vast incarcerations of the Holocaust and the Gulag. At the same time, the United States continued to increase its prison population, regarding incarceration as the common solution for crime. These trends that began a century ago resulted in the record-high proportion of U.S. citizens incarcerated today, compared to a much lower incarceration rate throughout modern Europe.

THE U.S. FEDERAL PRISON SYSTEM AND ALCATRAZ

The U.S. Congress decided to enter the prison business in 1891. Prior to this, states and local communities built and maintained all the prisons and jails. In 1929, the U.S. federal government established the Federal Bureau of Prisons, which worked to create similar standards for all federal prisons.

The prohibition of liquor in the 1920s created a major crime wave and swelled the population of federal prisons. It also led to the growth of

organized crime on a larger and more violent scale than had been seen before. To deal with the increase in hardcore criminals, the federal government decided to create a "prison of last resort." This prison would not attempt to rehabilitate inmates, because the offenders sent there were "vicious and irredeemable." This new prison would be designed with one sole purpose—to make sure no one ever escapes. They almost succeeded in this goal. The government constructed this "prison of last resort" off the coast of San Francisco, California, on Alcatraz Island.

Alcatraz Prison sits on a rocky island.

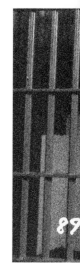

Cell block inside Alcatraz

From 1850 to 1933, Alcatraz was a military fort; it became a federal prison on January 1, 1934, remaining so until its closure in 1963. During its twenty-nine years of operation, Alcatraz never officially recognized a single successful escape; however, some historians believe three inmates, Frank Morris and John and Clarence Anglin, did escape. The 1962 motion picture, *Escape from Alcatraz*, portrayed their efforts. No one has seen or heard of the three men since they left "The Rock" (Alcatraz's informal name), and prison authorities recorded them "presumed drowned." Yet others wonder: Was that due more to the pride prison authorities had in an "inescapable prison" than to facts? Forty years later, the television show *Mythbusters* constructed a raft from rubber raincoats, like the raft presumed to be used by the escapees, and successfully paddled it at night to the nearby Marin Headlands, thus proving the "inescapable rock" of Alcatraz may have had three escapees after all.

INCARCERATION ON A VAST SCALE: THE HOLOCAUST, JAPANESE INTERNMENT, AND THE GULAG

In the middle of the twentieth century, Germany and Russia created death camps that were vast and utter nightmares, while the United States relocated thousands of Japanese Americans to internment camps. This book focuses on incarceration as punishment for crimes, but here we'll take a brief look at political imprisonment.

Japanese Americans stand in line to enter an internment center in California during World War II.

During the Holocaust, mass murders were routinely performed at the prison camp of Auschwitz.

The word "Holocaust" denotes the attempt by the Nazi Party in Germany, before and during World War II, to exterminate all persons deemed "undesirable" by the party. The Nazis murdered more than six million Jews, plus gypsies, communists, homosexuals, prisoners of war, and political opponents. No one is sure of the numbers, but historians believe the Nazis killed between ten and fourteen million people in the Holocaust. The primary tools for this mass slaughter were the death camps—

Prisoners at the Buchenwald concentration camp during the Holocaust.

Forced labor in the Russian Gulag

massive facilities designed to incarcerate men, women, and children for the purposes of slave labor or death in gas chambers and cremation afterward. The death camps were also factories, and Nazi workers processed even the corpses of their victims to create products for the war effort. The world will forever remember the Holocaust as one of the worst episodes of cruelty in all of human history.

"Thou shalt not be a victim. Thou shalt not be a perpetrator. Above all, thou shalt not be a bystander."
—from the Holocaust Museum in Washington, D.C.

World War II was also the cause of massive confinement of an ethnic group within the United States. After Japanese forces attacked Pearl Harbor in Hawaii, and fearing Japanese Americans would "spy" for the enemy, the U.S. government rounded up thousands of Japanese Americans and confined them to internment camps, where they lived throughout the war. During the internment, the government took precautions to protect the property of those forced to move. They indexed and warehoused the personal possessions of Japanese American citizens and issued receipts to the owners. Despite such attempts to protect their properties, however, many families still suffered losses resulting from the internment.

From 1930 to 1953, Russia ran the Gulag, a system of forced labor camps in Siberia, used mostly for political prisoners who opposed the Soviet state. More than a million people died in these camps. Forced to do harsh labor logging or mining, underfed and poorly sheltered, 80 percent of prisoners died during their first months in the Gulag.

PRISON RIOTS IN THE UNITED STATES, 1950–1970

Throughout the second half of the twentieth century, the American incarceration rate continued to climb. In 1925, there were 93,000 inmates in the United States, but by 1950, the number had risen to 166,000 and by 1970, 196,000. As numbers increased, so did problems. Prisons and jails routinely held more inmates than they were built to house; and disease, prisoner abuse, gang violence, rape, and other problems increased accordingly.

Worsening prison conditions caused riots. Between 1950 and 1966, over a hundred riots occurred in U.S. prisons. As Blake McKelvey writes in his book *American Prisons*, "Locked in overcrowded prisons, often two or more in a cell scarcely adequate for one, the convicts needed no outside proof of their hardships. Yet news of a riot in one institution often served as the catalyst elsewhere." In 1952, riots broke out in Walla Walla, Washington; Trenton, New Jersey; and Jackson, Michigan, prisons. The Jackson riot was the worst; the largest prison in the nation at the time, it was so overcrowded the warden was using inmates to guard other inmates—a situation that practically set up conditions for the riot. Led by a

Psychiatric problems are common in prisons.

psychopathic inmate, prisoners took a dozen guards hostage and seized control of several blocks of the facility. In the end, all the hostages were unharmed and only one inmate died; it was a relatively peaceful end to a frightening situation.

The prison riots of the 1950s attracted public attention to prisoners' grievances, yet two decades later, conditions in most prisons had only worsened as overcrowding and underfunding continued. The two worst prison riots in U.S. history occurred in 1971, at Attica State Prison in New York, and 1980, in New Mexico. At Attica, more than 1,000 inmates took forty prison workers hostage, protesting what they said was "ruthless brutalization and disregard for the lives of the prisoners here and throughout the United States." Governor Nelson Rockefeller ordered state authorities to retake control of the facility, and on September 13, state police attacked, firing more than 2,200 rounds of live ammunition. The governor later stated that state troopers had done "a fine job" in the situation, yet ten hostages and twenty-nine inmates died in the attack; all the hostages died from gunfire from police and prison guards. Troopers stripped surviving inmates and beat them with clubs after retaking the facility. The aftermath of the Attica riot produced mixed results. **Conservatives** in the state's Republican Party lauded the governor's tough actions; the state of New York paid more than $8 million in damages to prisoners abused by troopers; and the Attica facility remains overcrowded. Nine years later, another prison riot, at the New Mexico State Penitentiary, left thirty-six people dead.

INCARCERATION NATION

At the start of the twenty-first century, the United States leads all other nations in incarceration. According to Bureau of Justice statistics, the U.S. prison population, already the largest in the world, reached a new high of more than 2.1 million in 2004, with 1 in every 138 residents of the country incarcerated, and an average of 932 new inmates entering the prison system every week. This costs U.S. taxpayers approximately $18 billion each year and causes significant overcrowding, with half of all U.S.

Each prisoner costs the American taxpayer thousands of dollars.

prisons holding more than the number of inmates they were designed to house. At the same time, blacks are incarcerated far more than people of other races; in 2004, 12.6 percent of black males in their late twenties were in prison, compared to only 3.6 percent of Hispanics and 1.7 percent of whites.

A trend in the early twenty-first century United States is "privatization" of prisons. Thirty-nine states hire private firms to provide such services as medical treatment, drug treatment, education, and staff training; and twenty-eight states allow private firms to operate prison facilities.

Supporters of privatization say private firms provide better prisons at less expense to taxpayers. Critics claim the "criminal justice industrial complex" encourages a harmful policy of incarcerating too many people.

The United States contrasts with other nations in terms of massive incarceration. The current incarceration rate in the United States is 726 inmates per 100,000 citizens. In Britain it's 142 per 100,000, in China 118, in France 91, in Japan 58, and in Nigeria 31, according to the Justice Policy Institute, an independent research organization. The high incarceration rate in the United States also contrasts with that of its neighbor to the north. Canada's incarceration rate, according to one recent survey, is 116 per 100,000 citizens.

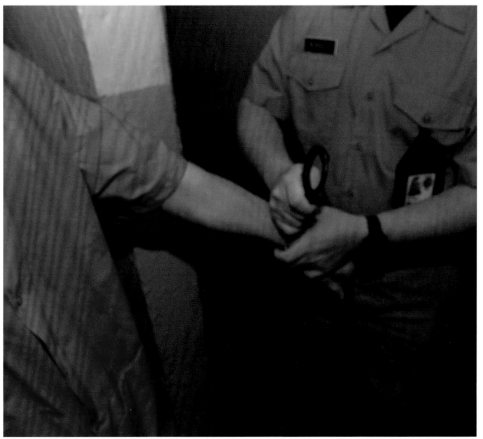

In many prisons, private companies pay guards' salaries.

Americans prefer to incarcerate wrongdoers.

Social scientists point out that having less people in prison does not mean a nation treats their citizens more humanely. Some countries in Asia, Latin America, and Africa violate human rights while they also boast a small prison population. They do this in several ways; some nations keep prisoners "unofficially," thus lowering the reported rate of incarceration and allowing the government to abuse these undocumented prisoners. Other nations still resort to public forms of punishment—such as whipping, cutting off fingers, or beheading—that were abandoned in Europe and North America more than a century ago. In a few Central American and African nations, persons opposed to the government have "disappeared," their lifeless bodies turning up later in rivers, garbage dumps, or shallow graves.

The United States prefers incarceration to other available choices. For more than a century, Europe and Canada have placed more emphasis on alternatives to prison such as probation, rehabilitation programs, and **community service** assignments for offenders. The fact that the United States leads the world in incarceration is largely due to public attitudes; current U.S. policies emphasize the need to "get tough on crime," especially drug-related crimes. In 2003, nearly 75 percent of offenders sentenced to time in state prisons were guilty of nonviolent crimes, and 51 percent of state inmates were serving time for nonviolent crimes. The same year, 22 percent of all federal and state U.S. inmates were serving time for drug-related offenses. Supporters of heavy incarceration policies claim locking up so many offenders has lowered the U.S. crime rate, while critics say massive imprisonment wastes taxpayers' money and will create more crime in the future. They allege that overcrowded prisons cause inmates to become hardened in crime.

CONCLUSIONS AND QUESTIONS

How should society treat persons who violate its laws? For 3,000 years, people have struggled with this question, and our modern-day prison

How should prisoners be treated?

systems reflect the ways people in the past have answered it. In democracies such as the United States and Canada, incarceration policies depend on the values of their citizens.

Do you believe prisons should rehabilitate prisoners, or punish them? Do the prisons in your country make you feel safer, or are these facilities hardening prisoners to commit more crimes in the future? Is it important to treat offenders humanely, or do lawbreakers deserve unpleasant and unsafe living conditions? These are important questions because you will be a voting citizen, and your values will influence the future of the prison system in your country.

GLOSSARY

acquitted: Declared by a court to be not guilty.

barbarism: Characteristics including unacceptable behavior, ignorance, and crudeness.

blasphemy: Showing disrespect for God or sacred things.

capital punishment: Punishment by death.

chivalry: The knightly code of conduct common in the Middle Ages.

city-states: Powerful, independent cities and the territory that surrounds them.

community service: A sentence given for a minor crime that involves performing a service for the community.

concubines: Women contracted to men in some societies to serve as sexual partners without the legal benefits of marriage.

conservatives: People who support political policies that tend to maintain traditional institutions and ways of doing things, while resisting change.

corporal punishment: Punishment that involves inflicting pain to the body.

Crusades: Military campaigns undertaken by Christians and sanctioned by the pope against Muslims between the eleventh and thirteenth centuries.

decapitation: Cutting off a person's head.

dehumanizing: Depriving the essential human qualities of mind, body, and spirit.

derision: Contempt and mockery.

espoused: Adopted or supported something as a belief or cause.

fetters: Shackles for the feet or ankles.

Great Depression: A drastic decline in the world economy resulting in mass unemployment and widespread poverty that lasted from approximately 1929 until 1939.

Gulag: The network of forced-labor camps used especially for political dissidents in the former Soviet Union.

heresy: Disagreement with beliefs of the church.

idealists: People who believe that perfection can be achieved and are satisfied with nothing less.

impregnable: Too strong to be captured or opened by force.

Near East: The part of the Middle East that is closest to countries of the Western world.

organized crime: Criminal activities that are widespread and centrally controlled.

pacifist: One who does not believe in violence or war as a means of settling disputes.

penology: The study of criminal treatment and incarceration.

premeditated: Planned.

repent: To feel sorry for deeds such as crimes.

sadistic: Delight in inflicting pain on others.

secular: Not controlled by a religious body or concerned with religious or spiritual matters.

spiritualist: A believer in spiritualism, which held that the dead could communicate with the living.

uncouth: Unrefined, crude.

Victorian Era: The time during the nineteenth-century reign of Queen Victoria in England, which was characterized by tight moral restrictions on sexuality and other social practices.

FURTHER READING

Christianson, Scott. *Condemned: Inside the Sing Sing Death House*. New York: New York University Press, 2000.

Kent, Peter. *Go to Jail! A Look at Prisons Through the Ages*. Brookfield, Conn.: Millbrook, 1998.

Miklos, Lacey. *Prisons and Jails: A Deterrent to Crime?* Farmington Hills, Mich.: Gale, 2004.

Morris, Norval, and David J. Rothman. *The Oxford History of the Prison: The Practice of Punishment in Western Society*. New York: Oxford University Press, 2005.

Rabiger, Joanna. *Daily Prison Life*. Broomall, Pa.: Mason Crest, 2003.

Solzhenitsyn, Alexander. *One Day in the Life of Ivan Denisovich*. New York: Signet Books, 1998.

Tower Oliver, Marilyn. *Alcatraz Prison in American History*. Berkeley Heights, N.J.: Enslow, 1998.

Townsend, John. *Prisons and Prisoners: Painful History of Crime*. Oxford, England: Raintree, 2005.

THE HISTORY OF INCARCERATION

FOR MORE INFORMATION

Alcatraz Island (National Park Service site)
www.nps.gov/alcatraz

Black Hoods and Iron Gags: The Quaker Experiment at Eastern State
Penitentiary in Philadelphia
www.missioncreep.com/mw/estate.html

The Chateau d'If: Visit and Pictures
www.plume-noire.com/feature/thecountofmontecristo/
chateaudif.html

Code of Hammurabi (online encyclopedia entry)
encyclopedia.lockergnome.com/s/b/Code_of_Hammurabi

A Guide to Prison Privatization
www.heritage.org/Research/Crime/BG650.cfm

History of New York States Prisons
www.geocities.com/MotorCity/Downs/3548/history.html

Incarcerated America: Human Rights Watch
www.hrw.org/backgrounder/usa/incarceration/

Prison History
www.notfrisco.com/prisonhistory/

Publisher's note:
The Web sites listed on this page were active at the time of publication.
The publisher is not responsible for Web sites that have changed their
addresses or discontinued operation since the date of publication. The
publisher will review and update the Web-site list upon each reprint.

BIBLIOGRAPHY

The American Correctional Association. *The American Prison from the Beginning: A Pictorial History.* College Park, Md.: Author, 1983.

Attica Prison Riot
http://www.pbs.org/wgbh/amex/rockefellers/peopleevents/e_attica.html.

Castle Dungeons
http://www.castles-of-britain.com/castlesg.htm.

Color of Justice (Black Commentary)
http://www.mindfully.org/Reform/2005/Color-Of-Justice27mar05.htm.

Hammurabi's Code
http://eawc.evansville.edu/anthology/hammurabi.htm.

Incarcerated America (Human Rights Watch)
http://www.hrw.org/backgrounder/usa/incarceration.

The Inquisition
http://www.religiousbook.net/Books/Online_books/Sh/Heart_21.html.

Joan of Arc in Prison
http://schoolweb.missouri.edu/linncntyr1.k12.mo.us/1jury/joan/treatmen.htm.

McKelvey, Blake. *American Prisons: A History of Good Intentions.* Glen Ridge, N.J.: Patterson Smith, 1993.

Morris, Norval, and David Rothman, eds. *The Oxford History of the Prison: The Practice of Punishment in Western Society.* New York: Oxford University Press, 1997.

Prison Privatization
http://www.heritage.org/Research/Crime/BG650.cfm.

INDEX

PICTURE CREDITS

Ben Stewart: pp. 96, 98, 99, 100, 101, 102
City of Marseille: p. 45
iStock: pp. 31, 66, 68, 70, 89, 90, 92
Library of Congress: pp. 78, 80
National Archives and Records Administration: pp. 91, 93
Penn Library: p. 59
photos.com: pp. 21, 26, 35, 36, 76, 87

To the best knowledge of the publisher, all other images are in the public domain. If any image has been inadvertently uncredited, please notify Harding House Publishing Service, Vestal, New York 13850, so that rectification can be made for future printings.

Chapter opening art was taken from a painting titled *Sardine Can Prison* by Raymond Gray.

Raymond Gray has been incarcerated since 1973. Mr. Gray has learned from life, and hard times, and even from love. His artwork reflects all of these.